# Little Puff

Modern Curriculum Press
**BEGINNING
TO
READ**
Series

# Little Puff

**Margaret Hillert**

Illustrated by Sid Jordan

LITTLE PUFF

ISBN 0-8136-5014-3   Hardbound

ISBN 0-8136-5514-5   Paperback          13 14 15 16 17 18 19 20     04 03 02 01 00

See me.
Big, big me.
Look at big red me.

See my little cars.
One, two, three.
One blue car.
One yellow car.
And one that is red.

6

But no one is here with me.
I do not like it here.
I guess I will look for something.

Here I go.
Jump, jump, jump to see what I
can see.

8

I can puff, puff, puff.
I can go away.
Away, away, away.

9

Puff—puff—.
Here I go.
Up—and up—and up!

Puff, puff.
Here I come.
Down,
down,
down,
down,
down.

11

Here comes something.
Look at this.
Look at this.
What is it?

12

We do not want you.
You can not come in here.
Go away.

Oh, no!
Look at this!
You can not do this!

Get away.
Get away.
This will not work.
We do not want you here.

Where can I go?
No one wants me.
Where can I go now?

16

What is this?
It looks like fun.
I guess I will go in here.

Oh, my.
What do I see here?
It is something big, big, big.

18

And look up here.
Look up, up, up.
Here is a big one, too.
A big one with spots.

Oh, oh.
Look in here.
Here is something funny.
The funny little ones can play.

20

Look at the mother.
A little one is with the mother.
I like this little one.

Oh, Little Puff.
Come here. Come here.
Help, help.
We want you.
You can help us.

You can work for us.
You can play with us.
We can ride with you.
What fun! What fun!

Ride with me.
Come ride with me.
Get in, get in, get in.

Now, this is fun.
I like it here.
I like this work.
This is the spot for me.

Margaret Hillert, author of several books in the MCP Beginning-To-Read Series, is a writer, poet, and teacher.

## LITTLE PUFF

A little red train finds a friendly place where children are looking for a train to ride. The story is told in 60 preprimer words.

**Word List**

| | | | |
|---|---|---|---|
| **5** see | that | **8** go | **14** oh |
| me | is | jump | **15** get |
| big | **7** but | to | work |
| look (s) | no | what | **16** where |
| at | here | can | now |
| red | with | **9** puff | **17** fun |
| **6** my | I | away | **19** too |
| little | do | **10** up | spot (s) |
| car (s) | not | **11** come (s) | **20** funny |
| one (s) | like | down | play |
| two | it | **12** this | **21** the |
| three | guess | **13** we | mother |
| blue | will | want (s) | **22** help |
| yellow | for | you | us |
| and | something | in | **23** ride |